CASE NO. 107

Case No. 107
Written by Pranjal Verma
Print Edition

First Published in India in 2021
Inkfeathers Publishing
New Delhi 110095

All rights reserved.

ISBN 978-93-90882-40-3

www.inkfeathers.com

CASE NO. 107

PRANJAL VERMA

Inkfeathers Publishing

DISCLAIMER

The contents of this book are solely owned by the Author of this book and are in no way intended to hurt anyone's religious, political, spiritual, brand, personal or fanatic beliefs and/or faith, whatsoever.

Unless otherwise indicated, all the names, characters, objects, businesses, places, events, incidents- whether physical/nonphysical, real/unreal, tangible/ intangible in whatsoever description used in this book are either the product of the author's imagination or used in a fictitious manner. Any resemblance to actual persons, objects, characters, names, entities, living or dead, or actual events is purely coincidental.

In case, any sort of plagiarism is detected within this book or in case of any complaints or grievances or objections, the publisher shall not be held responsible whatsoever.

CONTENTS

CASE NO. 107

CHAPTER ONE

Felicious — *A Delicious food Restaurant, Divynagar*

"After so long, we are having dinner together," said Priya.

"Yes, not only it's the professional relationship at work, but we are also more like a family." rejoiced Lakshman.

"Yes! You are right Lakshman. We are more like a family, working and spending time together. It's great!" stated Hina.

"Exactly," agreed Dev, "Now why not order some food" he said.

"Of course, what would you like to have today?" asked Priya.

"Why not Italian, what do you think Dev?" questioned Hina.

"Great idea, Hina! Let's have Italian then" he answered.

"Okay, then I am ordering Italian food" said Lakshman.

Having some chit-chat, they completed dinner and now it was time to leave.

"Well, it was a great time with you all" stated Hina.

"Indeed! I enjoyed every bit, especially the food" agreed Priya.

"Yeah, but now it's time to leave" continued Lakshman.

"Yes, see you guys tomorrow then" added Dev.

"Yes! But be on time, everyone" said Hina with a serious face.

"Chill," said Dev keeping a hand around her shoulder. "We will all be on time ma'am" he chuckled.

"Okay, whatever" she rolled her eyes. "But please be on time as the paperwork is pending" she commanded.

"Yes ma'am," they all spoke together and laughed.

"Okay, can we go now?" asked Dev.

"Of course," she responded.

"See you in the morning then," waved Dev and they all drove to their houses.

***

11th August, Divynagar, the bureau of Crime Unit. Four detectives were on duty at the moment: Senior Inspector Hina Chaturvedi, Senior Inspector Dev Sharma, Inspector Priya Khandelwal, and Sub Inspector Lakshman Gautam.

Suddenly the phone rang, Senior Inspector Hina attended the call, someone from Havai Apartments was on the line, flat no. 702, 5th floor.

Ritu, who worked as a maid in the house where the owner was murdered, had contacted the Crime Unit. Hina asked Dev to investigate the case with her and they were about to leave but the phone rang again. Inspector Priya Khandelwal attended the call, on the line Mrs. Shiny was speaking from the same building, Havai Apartments; flat no. 185, 2nd floor where her neighbour was murdered. Priya reported her seniors and Sub-Inspector Lakshman. Dev and Hina were surprised to hear that both murders had taken place in the same building. Dividing themselves into two teams, Senior Inspector Hina and Sub-Inspector Lakshman made their way to the 5th floor, whereas Senior Inspector Dev and Inspector Priya to the 2nd floor. The four detectives left for the crime spots.

CHAPTER TWO

Hina and Lakshman stepped into flat no. 702, 5th floor. It was the flat where Ritu worked as a maid. They saw a girl lying on the floor, dead. The detectives had put their gloves on. Hina checked the dead body. It had red spots all over.

"I think she's poisoned," presumed Hina.

There was a bouquet kept on the table of the living room. The dead body was sent to the forensic laboratory along with the bouquet.

The inquiry began.

"Who saw the dead body first?" questioned Hina.

"Ma'am I had seen Natasha Miss's body and contacted the Crime Unit" answered Ritu.

"So, you work here as a maid. At what time do you come here every day?" interrogated Lakshman.

"Miss Natasha leaves for office at 8am. So, I come at 7 am. Miss Natasha has given me a duplicate key in case I come late."

"Where does Natasha work?" interrogated Hina.

"I am sorry, I don't know" apologized Ritu.

"Thank you for your cooperation. If we need your help, we will contact you" said Lakshman and the two detectives left.

They were near the stairs, and someone had followed them.

"Excuse me," a voice called, and they turned to see who was there.

"There's something you need to know more about Natasha…" stated Mr. Kunwar, from flat 701.

"Yes…." acknowledged Hina.

"Natasha doesn't live alone. She lives with her parents—"

"But where are they?" asked Lakshman; "We didn't find them at the crime scene."

"Sir aunt and uncle are in Haridwar for vacation, they will return by the 17th" he replied.

"When did they leave for Haridwar?" questioned Hina.

"They left on 9th August; the day before yesterday" he replied.

"Thank you," said Hina, and the two detectives left.

Meanwhile, Dev and Priya investigated the 2nd murder, as they entered flat no. 185, 2nd floor; they saw a girl on the sofa, dead.

While examining the dead body Priya neither found any injury nor any other sign of death. What they found was only a glass of water on the table. The dead body along with the glass was sent to the forensic laboratory.

When Mrs. Shiny was questioned about her neighbour's details and how the murder took place, all she said was—

"She's Amrita. She works at AVP Call Centre. We were supposed to go shopping today. She took a leave for the special day planned by us. Apart from being neighbours, we are quite good friends, so we plan holidays like these often. In the morning when I called, she didn't answer, so I rang the doorbell, again there wasn't any response. Then I waited for her maid, Savitri as she has the duplicate keys of her house. We opened the door and saw Amrita was no more."

Savitri was present there. So, they took her statement as well—

"As Mrs. Shiny said, I am her maid, Savitri. Amrita ma'am has given me a duplicate key of her house in case I am late because she leaves for her office early and I reach here by 8. Sometimes our timings intersect with each other."

On further inquiry the detectives got to know that Amrita lived with her parents, they were on a vacation in Haridwar, and they left on 9th August.

CHAPTER THREE

The four detectives were on their way back to the bureau.

"Flat 702, 5th floor, I suppose Natasha's poisoned because there were red spots all over her body and a bouquet," said Hina.

"Amrita's murder, flat 185, 2nd floor; There was no sign of death, no injury, nothing. Just a glass of water on the table..." stated Dev.

"And the victims' parents are enjoying a vacation in Haridwar," added Priya.

"I find these maids, Ritu and Savitri, suspicious. These two have the duplicate keys of the house. They can enter the house anytime they want, these two can be involved in the murder" suspected Lakshman.

Meanwhile, they reached and walked into the bureau.

"Lakshman find out the details of the hotel in which Amrita and Natasha's parents are staying and call them here as soon as possible" ordered Hina.

"Priya keep a strict eye on these maids, what they do, whom they meet, phone calls and everything, I want each detail" commanded Dev.

"Yes," they both followed and left for the assigned work.

Dev and Hina entered the forensic lab.

"Hello" greeted Dr. Swaraj.

"Hello sir, please give some more information about the dead bodies of Amrita and Natasha," said Hina.

"Yes..., continued Dr. Niharika, the bouquet that was found on Natasha's table is the murder weapon. It contained aconite leaves along with the flowers. Aconite is a poison that is derived from the plant Monkshood. The red spots which we see all over Natasha's body. That's the only post-mortem sign, asphyxia. It causes arrhythmic heart functioning which leads to suffocation. Poisoning can occur right after touching the leaves of the plant. We have found traces of aconite on her fingertips. She touched the leaves and died. Along with that, there's a small tag inside this bouquet which says 'Apar's Bouquet House'."

"We have to visit this bouquet shop," said Hina.

"Amrita's murder, doctor," said Dev.

"She is poisoned, there is no sign of poison on the upper body, but we found arsenic in her stomach. That glass of water had arsenic mixed in it. Arsenic is a poison that doesn't change the colour of food or water when mixed. It is also referred to as 'The King of Poisons' for its discreteness and potency. It doesn't leave any sign on the upper body. She had consumed that water" elucidated Dr. Swaraj.

"Talking about the timing of deaths, Amrita lost her consciousness between 7:30 to 8:00 am whereas Natasha died at 7:50 am, that's it," said Dr. Niharika.

"Thank you, doctors," said Dev, and they moved out of the forensic Lab.

CHAPTER FOUR

The Next Day

As they walked into the bureau Lakshman was shuffling through some documents. "Yes, Lakshman, any details?" asked Hina.

"Ma'am, their parents were staying at 'Hotel Ganga Basin' in Haridwar. We have informed them to reach the bureau. They will be here any moment."

"Great job" applauded Dev.

A few minutes later, four elderly people rushed into the bureau, sobbing, and mourning for the deceased ones. The officers were working in their places. Listening to them mourn, they immediately got off their seats and tried to calm them down.

"What happened to our kids? Who did this to our kids?" asked a woman sobbing.

"Please calm down," Priya offered her water.

"Ma'am these are the victims' parents, the couple on the right are Natasha's parents, Mrs. Ileana and Mr. Shakti whereas the couple on the left are Amrita's parents, Mrs. Vaishnavi and Mr. Neeraj," said Lakshman.

"I am really sorry. I am aware that it is a tough time for you. But your answers will help the investigation...," said Dev.

"Yes, continue officers" agreed Mr. Shakti, sobbing.

"Okay. So, did Amrita and Natasha have had any fights in the past few days? Do they have any enemies?" questioned Hina.

"No, they didn't fight with anyone in the past few days—" answered Mrs. Ileana.

"And they have no enemies" continued Mrs. Vaishnavi.

"Fine. You all were staying at the same hotel in Haridwar 'Hotel Ganga Basin', do you know each other or was it a coincidence?" asked Dev.

"We know each other, and our daughters are very close friends. We had planned this vacation together" replied Mr. Neeraj.

"Thank you for your cooperation. We'll contact you if we require further information.

You can leave now," said Dev.

"Lakshman you may drop them to their homes safely" ordered Hina.

"Priya, any progress?" asked Dev.

"Sir, those maids have been spied on and we even have their call records, Amrita's maid Savitri went to a shop 'Pure Water Suppliers' and paid the due amount, they supply water to

Amrita's house, and they might have mixed arsenic in the water," replied Priya.

"Yeah, we have to go to this 'Pure Water Suppliers' now. Anyway, you continue" said Hina.

"Speaking of the call records, everything's fine there. Both the maids have either called Amrita, Natasha, and other people where they work or their family members. And Ritu is fine, no trouble with these two," she added.

"Good," praised Hina. "Now we must go to AVP Call Centre and Pure Water Suppliers, move" she ordered.

The four detectives moved out of the bureau and drove to the locations.

CHAPTER FIVE

8:45 in the morning, the same day

Dev and Priya reached the AVP Call Centre.

"Crime Unit" Dev showed his identity card.

"Amrita works here, right?" asked Priya.

"Yes, I am the President of this Call Centre, Swati. Amrita works here but—"

"Now don't tell us she's on leave or not here," said Dev.

"Umm… yes sir but how do you know she's not here" mumbled Swati.

All of a sudden someone came screaming.

"Swati ma'am, Natasha also didn't come today without informing."

"Who are you?" asked Priya.

"I am the manager here, Zoya," she said.

"Aah, Natasha also didn't come today, huh…" Swati sighed.

"Wait, what! Natasha also works here?" exclaimed Priya.

"Yes, do you know her?" asked Zoya.

"Amrita and Natasha, two employees of your Call Centre have been murdered," rasped Dev.

"Seriously!?" Swati exclaimed; her mouth wide open.

"Do we seem to be joking?" hurled Priya.

"Sorry," she apologized.

"Anyway, tell us something about them. Did they seem tense for the past few days?" interrogated Dev.

"They were very hard-working young girls. But this habit of taking leaves without informing was something I didn't like very much," said Swati.

"They weren't tensed but were quite cheerful, I heard them planning about some vacation for their parents" added Zoya.

"Thank you," said Priya, and they left.

In the meantime, Hina and Lakshman were at the Pure Water Suppliers.

"Yesterday who supplied water to Amrita's house?" questioned Hina.

"Ma'am it was Anupam, yesterday he supplied water to her house" responded the manager, Javed.

"Where is he?" asked Lakshman.

In the ongoing conversation, Hina espied a man running from the staff. She chased him half a mile and held him by his collar. She dragged him into the staff room.

"You seem to be in a haste Anupam. Were you about to board a train?" ranted Hina.

"Actually…umm... I forgot my cell phone at home" he stammered.

"So, is this your neighbour's phone in the pocket?" questioned Lakshman.

"Aah! It's here. I have been searching for it since morning" he rejoiced.

"We could think something better, if you would've made a better excuse" she laughed.

"Now tell why did you poison the water being supplied to Amrita's house?" demanded Hina.

"No, I haven't poisoned the water…I am innocent…. please leave me" bawled Anupam.

"Oh really! Are you going to speak up or do you need some help?" asked Lakshman, rolling up his sleeves.

"I was offered some money by a lady and a bottle of arsenic to mix in the water being supplied to Amrita's house. The money made me greedy..." gulped Anupam.

"'Money made me greedy,' every offender's key dialogue;" said Hina.

"Arrest him" she ordered.

The detectives were driving to the bouquet shop. Lakshman told Dev and Priya about Anupam.

"He's just a pawn of the game," said Hina.

They reached the bouquet shop and stepped inside.

CHAPTER SIX

"Yes, which bouquet do you prefer?" asked Apar, the owner.

"The bouquet which has poison" responded Dev.

"What!? We don't sell such bouquets!" he fumed.

"Crime Unit," said Hina, "See this bouquet, it contains a tag of your shop, it has been used as a murder weapon by putting aconite leaves in it."

"All the staff members should be here in a minute" ordered Priya.

Four men, wearing white shirts and brown pants, with a red cap on their head, stepped inside.

"Everyone's here" stated Apar.

Lakshman pointed out the third man from the left corner.

"Why are you sweating even in the air conditioner?" he questioned.

"It seems like the air conditioner isn't working properly, I think you should buy a new one Apar" added Dev.

"What happened Akshay? Are you alright?" asked Apar.

"Akshay—" said Priya. "Kumar?" she questioned.

"Malhotra, his full name is Akshay Malhotra" replied Apar.

Akshay was standing, staring at the floor, hands held tight one above another and sweat crossing his eyebrows. Lakshman and Dev pulled him from the corner and made him sit on a chair, shivers ran down his spine.

"Why did you put aconite leaves in Natasha's bouquet?" demanded Hina.

"I…. I was asked to do so…," he mumbled, "she offered me money and told me to put aconite leaves…bought the bouquet and went off."

"Who is she? Did you see her?" asked Dev.

"Her face was covered with a scarf, and she wore sunglasses," he stuttered.

Akshay was put behind the bars.

They returned to the bureau and two more murders were reported, Ashiana Apartments flat no. 1032 and 1034, 11th floor. Two more victims; Arishfa and Abhilasha, their neighbours contacted Crime Unit. The officers left for the crime scene, but the strange thing was Ashiana Apartments was next to Havai Apartments. The investigation was carried on.

2 in the Afternoon

Hina and Dev were in flat no. 1032 from where Abhilasha contacted. Abhilasha navigated Pragati's dead body, the owner who was shot in the head. Her body was laying on the floor, with splashes of blood all over. The dead body was sent to the forensic laboratory for the post-mortem report.

In flat 1034 Mitalya, again shot in the head, in the same way, right in the middle. The floor was stained with blood.

The officers inquired the neighbours.

"Priya, collect the fingerprints on Pragati and Mitalya's doorknobs and send those samples to the forensic lab" instructed Hina.

"Sure," she moved.

"Ms. Arishfa, how did you find Mitalya's dead body?" asked Dev.

"I was going to the market, around 1 pm," answered Arishfa. "I saw her door slightly open. I thought she must have forgotten to close it, so I rang the doorbell to call her out of the house. I even tried calling her, but she didn't answer, and in the end, I knocked at the door. I tried every means to contact her, then I thought if something's wrong and entered the house."

"And Pragati's body, Ms. Abhilasha?" questioned Hina.

"I came out of my house on hearing Arishfa's scream. This morning Pragati didn't go to her office and even didn't appear after listening to such noise. We called her, knocked at the door, and tried to connect to her but she wasn't responding. So, we called the security guard to unlock her door and saw she's dead" responded Abhilasha.

"And ma'am the trophy that was kept on the shelf in Mitalya's living room is not there" informed Arishfa.

"Which trophy?" asked Priya.

"Mitalya won a trophy as 'The Best Student' in her college," said Arishfa.

CHAPTER SEVEN

"Lakshman search the house" ordered Priya. He nodded. On searching the house Lakshman didn't find any trophy but something strange.

"Ma'am, I found this keyring under the bed, with an 'A', I think this might be the initial of the culprit" he stated.

"Yes, you are right. This could be the initial of the culprit, maybe accidently it slipped from the culprit's pocket, or it broke and fell off, unnoticed by the culprit" said Priya, examining the keyring.

"This is possible," agreed Hina, "Also, there's no point Mitalya having a keyring with a random letter from the alphabet, it surely belongs to the criminal," she added.

"Send this to the forensic laboratory, we might find the criminal's fingerprints if lucky" ordered Priya.

"Sure," responded Lakshman.

"Didn't any of you hear the sound of the gun, or at least when they shouted, didn't you hear any sound?" asked Dev.

"No sir, there was no sound—" said Arishfa.

"Yes, we didn't hear any sound," added Abhilasha.

"The criminal must have used a silencer," said Hina.

"You," Lakshman pointed at the guard, "did you find any strange human entering the society? Or any other person who seemed off?"

Umm…yes, two delivery boys entered the society, they said that they have to pick up return packages" he answered.

"Did you check their identity cards?" questioned Hina.

"Sorry, but no" he apologized.

"If you would have checked, today these two would not have murdered" she scolded.

"When did they enter the society?" she asked.

"Yesterday, 11 pm."

"Didn't you ask which parcels they wanted to pick up late at night?" asked Dev.

"Yes, I did but they said that was the time allotted by the customers"

"Oh my," she sighed.

"If you see them again, will you be able to recognise them?" asked Dev.

"Yes sir" he acknowledged. "Also, I saw a lady returning from Miss Mitalya's flat late at night" he added.

"Did you see her face?" asked Priya.

"No ma'am,"

"Where were you when she entered the building?" questioned Hina.

"Actually, I had gone at the tea stall to get some tea for myself, so that I don't dose off in the middle of my duty" replied the guard.

"So careless." fumed Hina.

"Didn't check the identity cards of the delivery boys and didn't see the lady entering the building" she added.

"Can you tell what time it was when she was returning?" asked Dev.

"It was 2:30 am" he replied.

"Someone whom you didn't see entering the building, returns from the building at 2:30 am and you don't even bother to ask why was she visiting Mitalya in odd hours. Great!" fumed Hina.

"I…I thought she was a friend…and was there to say hello" he stammered.

"Who the hell says Hello to a friend at 2:30 am and that too by visiting them," she scolded him.

"I am sorry, I will be alert now" he apologised.

"Lakshman, call the sketch artist and ask him to make the sketches with the help of this guard" ordered Dev.

They went to the bureau and went to the forensic laboratory.

CHAPTER EIGHT

5 in the evening

"Hello officers," greeted Dr. Niharika.

"Hello, Niharika. Do we know something about guns?" asked Hina.

"Yes, Pistol Auto 9mm 1A is used for Pragati's murder and Browning High Power Pistol is used in Mitalya's murder" she responded.

"Boss, when we talk about the timings, Pragati was shot at 11:10 pm and Mitalya at 11:15" added Dr. Swaraj.

"Apart from Pragati and Mitalya's fingerprints on their doorknobs, there are three different ones also" informed Dr. Niharika.

"Did you try matching them with our criminal records?" questioned Priya.

"Yes, two fingerprints have matched with Mahesh and Shyam, two contract killers."

"Mahesh and Shyam, two most wanted contract killers," said Hina

"And the third fingerprint doctor, whose is it?" asked Priya.

"We don't know whose it is, as it didn't match with our criminal records. The only information we have is that the fingerprint is of a lady" replied Dr. Niharika.

"Fingerprint of a lady, this means that the keyring could be of the lady who visited Mitalya at 2:30 am in night. There is a possibility of that lady's name starting with 'A' or it is not just a possibility, that lady's name begins with 'A'," said Hina.

"Yes, you are right," agreed Dev.

"Also, as per the reports, Mitalya and Pragati were dead before 12am, so it's clear that this lady didn't kill them" said Priya.

"Yes, but she could have given the contract" stated Lakshman.

"You are right" agreed Priya.

"And is there any fingerprint on the keyring?" asked Lakshman.

"No, we didn't find any fingerprint of the keyring" answered Dr. Swaraj.

"Fine," said Priya.

"Priya, take out every detail of Mahesh and Shyam, this time they'll be punished by law" ordered Hina.

She nodded and moved for searching their details as per the orders.

"And we shall see who is this miss A" stated Dev.

"Yes. Well, cool name given to that unknown lady whose name begins with 'A'. 'Miss A' sounds good" appreciated Hina.

"Thankyou" said Dev.

"Lakshman; ask Pragati and Mitalya's parents to reach the bureau" ordered Hina and the three of them moved out.

After a few minutes—

"Yes Lakshman, what about the sketches, are they ready?" questioned Dev.

"Sir, these are the sketches", Lakshman held him two papers.

The first man sketched was a bald, dark-skinned man with a sharp nose and moustache. The second man was a curly-haired, fair one with a beard, a long nose, and pierced ears.

Dev held the two sketches and observed them.

"If I am not wrong, then these are Mahesh and Shyam, right?" guessed Hina.

"Yes, you are right, these are Mahesh and Shyam," acknowledged Dev.

"So, both of them, dressed up as delivery boys, went into Ashiana Apartments and murdered Pragati and Mitalya" she stated.

"Exactly...," he said.

"And ma'am, after contacting Pragati and Mitalya's parents, we got to know that they are also in Haridwar, staying at Hotel Ganga Basin and they'll reach here by tomorrow morning," said Lakshman.

"This hotel is the same in which Natasha and Amrita's parents were staying, right?" asked Hina.

"Yes, I think these four murders are connected" responded Dev.

"Look," Priya called.

"Yeah," Hina moved towards her table and Lakshman and Dev followed her.

"I have found the phone number and address of these two contract killers, Mahesh and Shyam," said Priya.

"Proceed," acknowledged Dev.

"The phones are switched off and we cannot trace them. Now we are left with their addresses. They live in Adarsh Nagar, house no. 51 and 90."

"Good," praised Hina.

"Let's go then," said Dev.

CHAPTER NINE

They drove to Adarsh Nagar, which was 50 miles away from Divyanagar. They reached the location around 7 pm.

Priya rang the doorbell of house no. 51, an old lady opened the door who was presumably Mahesh's mother.

"We want to meet Mahesh," said Dev.

"He has gone out, but who are you?" she asked.

"Senior Inspector Dev and—"

"Inspector Priya, Crime Unit" added Priya.

"Priya search the house" ordered Dev.

She nodded and moved in.

"But why?" his mother asked as the inspector entered her home.

"Your son is one of the most wanted contract killers. Recently he has murdered a girl" answered Dev.

"Sir," Priya moved out holding a gun in her hands, "this gun was hidden in the closet."

"Do you know where he has gone?" he asked.

"No, he hasn't told me" she answered.

"We came here to arrest him, but either it's his luck or has he disappeared" grinned Priya.

"Fine, thank you," said Dev, and they moved out.

Hina and Lakshman were standing outside house no. 90. Hina rang the doorbell. A tall, dark-skinned lady, wearing a black velvet dress, rings on her fingers, and glasses hanging from her neck was sitting on the sofa reading a book. On hearing the doorbell, she stood up and opened the door, pushing her glasses on her nose, and came out of the house.

"Yes," she greeted, shrinking her nose, the book was still in her hand. "Who are you?"

"Crime Unit" answered Hina.

"Oh! Hello officers, Crime Unit, at my place. Is something wrong?" she whined.

"Can we meet Shyam?" asked Lakshman.

"What happened?" she asked.

"Is Shyam there? We want to meet him," fumed Hina.

"No," she smirked.

"Lakshman, search the house" ordered Hina.

"Do you have a search warrant?" she thundered.

"We don't need a search warrant to go through a criminal's house," replied Hina.

"Move on Lakshman," she said and stepped into the house. The lady caught Hina by the wrist and pulled her. They both stopped.

"Behave yourself," thundered Hina. "For interrupting an on-duty officer in investigation and for physical violence, you can be arrested. I guess you must know this as you were asking for the search warrant."

Hina tried to get off her wrist, but the lady insisted and didn't leave her. Meanwhile, Dev and Priya walked in.

"What's going on?" asked Dev.

Hina finally freed herself and stepped near them.

"She is interfering with the investigation," said Lakshman.

"Lakshman, you move in and search the house. Let's see if someone dares to stop us" ordered Priya.

Hina was standing, her hands folded.

"Yes, so what was the reason to stop me like that" she questioned.

"Yes, we also want to know the reason for this kind of behaviour with Hina," said Dev.

"You weren't listening to me—"

"Great. So, on that logic I would have hit you for interfering in our work, right?" retorted Hina.

"See, the reason we aren't saying something to you is that we respect you and you haven't done anything wrong," said Dev.

"Yes, and don't take advantage of that—" added Priya.

"Otherwise, we know how to do our work," Hina continued.

"Sorry," she apologized.

"Good," said Hina.

Lakshman moved out of the house. "Ma'am," he showed a gun, "this gun was under the bed."

"Now, would you like to say something?" asked Dev.

The lady stared at the floor.

"Anyway, do you know where Shyam is?" asked Hina.

"No,"

"Fine," said Priya, and they left.

"Well, what do you think about her?" asked Dev as they were walking.

"About whom?" questioned Hina.

"Shyam's mother," he replied.

"Oh my!" she sighed, "Don't talk about her. She's unpredictable, I mean what made her haul me like that."

Everyone laughed.

CHAPTER TEN

They were walking towards their car to proceed with the case.

After walking a few miles, they saw two men standing near a bike, facing away from them. One was bald and wearing a red shirt, the other one had curly hair and pierced ears, wearing a blue shirt. Lakshman unlocked the car and opened the door—

"Wait," ordered Priya.

"These men seem familiar, don't they?" she asked.

"Yeah, it feels like we have seen them somewhere" answered Dev.

"These are Mahesh and Shyam," said Hina.

The two men turned towards them.

"That's the Crime Unit" stammered Mahesh.

"Run for your life" shouted Shyam.

The officers ran behind them and after a rat-cat race, Hina and Dev caught each of them by their collars and dragged them towards their car.

"Mahesh and Shyam, most wanted criminals," said Dev.

"Finally, you are in custody" added Priya.

"Who gave you the contract to kill Mitalya and Pragati?" thundered Hina.

"A…Akanksha" stuttered Mahesh.

"Akanksha, who's this?" asked Lakshman.

"Just make sure you aren't lying" fumed Hina.

"No, we aren't," said Shyam.

"This name, Akanksha. We are hearing this for the first time in this case, right?" confirmed Dev.

"Yes, you are right" stated Priya.

"Arrest them," ordered Hina.

They arrested Mahesh and Shyam and drove to the bureau.

13th August, the next day—

"Mam, Pragati, and Mitalya's parents are on the way, and they will be here in the next 10 minutes" stated Priya.

"Okay. Have you found any mention of "Akanksha" in our criminal records?" asked Hina.

"No, ma'am," she answered.

"I think she's a new criminal," said Dev.

"Yes, it seems like that," agreed Hina. "Wait, I think she's our 'Miss A', a lady returns from Mitalya's house at 2:30 am, we found a keyring under her bed with the letter 'A' and Mahesh and Shyam said that Akanksha had given them the contract to kill Mitalya and Pragati. I am pretty sure this keyring belongs to Akanksha, and she is the lady who was spotted returning from Mitalya's house at 2:30 am" she continued.

"You are right, we found our 'Miss A'. Akanksha is the culprit" agreed Dev.

"But we don't have any details of this Akanksha" sighed Hina.

After a few minutes, two couples entered the bureau.

"I am Shreya, and he is my husband Ashok. Pragati is our daughter," said the couple on the left.

"I am Ellen, and he is my husband Ajay, we are Mitalya's parents," said the couple on the left.

Hina and Priya left their seats, moving forward to the inquiry.

"We are so sorry for what happened, but you have to answer some questions to keep the investigation going on so that the criminal can be found out," said Lakshman.

"Continue," agreed Mr. Ajay.

"Fine. Were your daughters, Pragati and Mitalya, tensed? Was there any change in their behaviour from the past few days?" questioned Priya.

"No—" answered Mrs. Ellen.

"They were alright—" added Mr. Ajay.

"They were happy—" continued Mr. Ashok.

"Because we were going on a vacation planned by them," completed Mrs. Shreya.

"Okay, do you know Natasha and Amrita?" asked Hina.

"Yes, they and our daughters are very close friends. We and their parents were on a vacation together in Haridwar," responded Mrs. Ellen.

"I am sure these four murders are connected," stated Dev.

"Yeah," agreed Lakshman.

"Where do Pragati and Mitalya work?" asked Hina.

"AVP Call Centre" replied Mrs. Shreya.

"Thank you, you can leave now" professed Priya.

Lakshman dropped them at their houses.

"This Call Centre is also connected to this case," said Priya.

"Yes, we should visit this centre again," stated Lakshman.

"Let's move then." ordered Dev.

CHAPTER ELEVEN

They reached AVP Call Centre and stepped inside.

"You are here, again" wondered Swati.

"Two more employees of your Call Centre, Pragati and Mitalya have been murdered," said Dev.

"They too!" exclaimed Zoya.

"They didn't appear at work for two days," said Swati.

"Did you try contacting them?" asked Priya.

"No, we assumed that they had taken a leave without informing us, as usual" hesitated Zoya.

"Great. Two members of your staff at your Call Centre haven't been coming to work for two days and you didn't even try contacting them" fumed Hina.

"Sorry" they apologized.

"What sorry?" asked Lakshman.

"Someone murders four employees of your Call Centre and nobody knows anything. You, Swati as being the President and

Zoya, the Manager. You both have the responsibility to check on your employees, don't you?" thundered Dev.

"We are very sorry; I swear this won't happen again," said Swati.

They were just stepping out, Priya overheard Zoya saying something to Swati, and she turned around.

"Ma'am, Akanksha emailed a leave application, it says she was out of the station and will return by today" informed Zoya.

"Do you know Akanksha?" asked Priya and the team turned around with her.

"Yes, she works here," answered Swati.

"Oh!" exclaimed Lakshman.

"We want her phone number and address along with her photo" ordered Hina.

"Yes, she lives in flat no. 25, 1st floor, Deluxxe Apartments, and her contact number is 7XX45XXX9X," answered Zoya.

Meanwhile, after shuffling through some documents, Swati passed Dev her photo. Akanksha was a tall, dark-skinned, beautiful girl with a sharp nose and short, brown hair.

They moved out of the Call Centre and saw Deluxxe Apartments was at walking distance from AVP Call Centre. As they were walking Hina stopped and looked up at the buildings around them. They all turned around.

"What happened?" asked Dev.

"These four buildings, Ashiana, Havai, AVP Call Centre, and Deluxxe Apartments are opposite to each other," she wondered.

"Well, I guess you mean to say that it made it easier for Akansha to sneak around in their households. Behind their backs, right?" he confirmed.

"Exactly…" she replied.

"Well, good observation skills" he complimented.

"I know," she replied.

They reached her house and Lakshman rang the doorbell.

"Priya, trace Akanksha's phone" ordered Dev.

"It's switched off" she answered.

"Don't stop trying until you find the location" ordered Hina.

An old man opened the door.

"Yes," he received them.

"You?" asked Lakshman.

"I am Lauren, Akanksha's father," he answered.

 "Crime Unit," introduced Priya.

"Can we meet Akanksha?" she asked.

"No, she's out of the station and hasn't returned yet" he responded.

"Priya and Lakshman, search the house" ordered Dev.

They moved inside, searched her house, and came out with four photos. Priya handed them to Hina.

"Anupam, Akshay—" said Dev pointing out at two photos.

"Mahesh and Shyam…" continued Hina as she took the rest two photos from Priya.

"I think the lady who bribed Anupam to add arsenic in Amrita's water and Akshay to add Aconite leaves to Natasha's bouquet, is Akanksha," said Dev.

"Yes," agreed Hina, "Did you find anything else?" she asked Lakshman.

"An empty bottle of Arsenic ma'am," he responded.

"It's clear that Akanksha is the criminal," stated Hina.

"Yes," agreed Dev.

"Thank you," said Lakshman to Akanksha's parents, and they left.

They moved towards the car and were driving to Divyanagar.

"We've found Akanksha's location," exclaimed Priya from the backseat.

"Where is she?" asked Hina, slowing down the car.

"In the temple, near Divyanagar" she answered.

"The most crowded temple?" questioned Dev.

"Yes sir," said Lakshman, glancing at the tablet.

"This girl is in danger now," asserted Hina, changing the gears.

CHAPTER TWELVE

They reached the temple and stepped in. Each one of them went in different directions. Hina saw Akanksha standing near the gate, she called Priya, and they both were slowly approaching her. She saw them coming and ran. They chased her midway down the road. Suddenly a black car came, she sat in it and went off. Priya called Dev and Lakshman. She asked them to come towards their car.

As they came Hina asked Dev to follow the black car whose number was 'MH4712'. While the bureau was a few miles away, they overtook Akanksha's car and stopped near the bureau.

Hina and Priya stepped out of the car. Priya held her by the wrist. Akanksha kicked her in the stomach and Priya fell against the car. Hina was standing behind Akanksha, she held her arm and twisted it. Priya stood up and was in front of her.

"You, okay?" asked Hina.

"Yeah," she responded.

They dragged her into the bureau and made her sit on a chair. She was being recorded. Lakshman and Priya were standing behind her, on either side. Dev and Hina at the front.

"What made you hire four different people for murdering Natasha, Amrita, Mitalya, and Pragati?" thundered Hina.

"What are you saying? Natasha, Amrita, Mitalya and Pragati have been murdered!" she exclaimed.

"Yes, now don't act innocent. We know that you hired four different people for murdering them," retorted Lakshman.

"Answer what has been asked," fumed Priya.

"Are you out of your mind? Why would I hire someone to murder them? If I got a chance, I would kill them with my own hands" she smirked.

"Wait you mean to say you haven't hired Akshay, Anupam, Mahesh and Shyam to murder them?" asked Dev.

"Yes, I am saying that if I got a chance, I would kill them with my own hands" she responded.

"How is this possible? Did you visit Mitalya's house late at night and returned at 2:30 am in night?" questioned Hina.

"Yes, I had gone there, but not to murder anyone," she stated.

"So would you tell us why did you go there?" asked Dev.

"To search for the trophy, I didn't find it, so I returned" she replied.

"You are saying that when you had gone to search for the trophy, you didn't find it. That means the trophy was stolen by someone before you entered Mitalya's house" said Hina.

"Yes, well that is what you heard" she retorted.

"I even saw Mitalya dead with a pool of blood on the floor, and I just cannot express how happy I am, but also sad because I wasn't able to kill her" she smirked.

"Why did you go there to steal the trophy and why are you so happy knowing that Amrita, Natasha, Mitalya and Pragati are dead?" fumed Hina.

"And we even found a keyring under the bed with the letter 'A' isn't it your initial? Was that keyring yours?" asked Dev.

"Firstly, there are more people whose name begins with an 'A', not just me in the universe. Secondly, you got your answer that I am not the criminal. So, be happy with it" she replied.

"Behave yourself," commanded Hina.

"And speak up why did you go there to steal the trophy and why are you so happy that Natasha, Amrita, Mitalya and Pragati are dead, and why you wish you would have killed them with your own hands" she demanded.

"What if I don't," she laughed.

"Well, then we have Hina and Priya for you. Am I right?" said Dev looking at them.

"Yes, we are here" answered Hina.

"What will you do, beat me? Well, try that as well because I am not going to open my mouth even a little bit" she giggled.

"Okay. So, don't. Why waste our time on you," said Hina.

"Yeah," said Dev and handed her a water bottle. "Have some water," he continued.

"Wow!" she cackled, loosening the cap of the bottle.

"First time in the Crime Unit's history, the officers weren't able to extract a confession from someone," she laughed.

CHAPTER THIRTEEN

They all started laughing.

"Why are you laughing?" she fumed and stood up pushing her chair back.

"Because one more criminal is going to lose her life" answered Priya.

"What do…you mean?" she asked.

"And didn't I tell you I am not a criminal?" she continued.

"The water you drank is from Amrita's house, the one which had Arsenic mixed in it, she was poisoned?" responded Dev.

"Yeah, she must be very happy knowing the fact Amrita was poisoned? In the next 10 minutes, you'll be lying on the floor" stated Hina.

"Well, committing crime is a sin for sure, but hiding it also makes you a criminal. You saw Mitalya's dead body and instead of contacting us, you just walked off and celebrated" fumed Priya.

"What?" she exclaimed. "You can't do this to me, this isn't fair. I mean…your job is to save people, to provide justice, that's why you are a part of the Crime Unit, how can you kill somebody?" she fumbled.

"We can," said Lakshman.

"No, you can't," she shouted. "I don't want to die, this isn't fair."

"Oh! So, what you did to those four girls was fair and what we are doing is unfair. Great!" fumed Dev.

"What made you even think that you can kill innocent people?" thundered Hina.

"They weren't innocent, and I didn't kill anyone," she sobbed and sat down.

"Then why Mahesh and Shyam gave us your name?" boomed Priya.

"I don't know" she shouted.

"Volume down," commanded Lakshman.

"So, are they lying? Mahesh and Shyam?" questioned Hina.

"Yes," she replied.

"We will deal with them later. You tell what is your connection with the victims and why you went at Mitalya's place to steal the trophy and why you wish you would have killed them" fumed Dev.

"We were in the same college. Natasha, Amrita, Pragati, and Mitalya were quite close friends. At some point, I used to be a part of their group. Our friendship was famous in college, from students to every teacher knew who we were, and our bond was really great. Everything was going well until that moment; while I was in my worst times, and they left me alone. We weren't friends anymore. That was forgivable, in fact, I was glad that I cut off toxicity from my life.

It was the last year of college. In our college, the 'Best Student of College' award is given to the one who's the best in academics and sports in the final year. Me and Mitalya were nominated for it. The best one was still to be chosen. I was pretty sure that Natasha, Amrita, and Pragati would try their best to help Mitalya win, and I was alert.

There were three weeks of further assessment based on which the best one was to be chosen. The first week was for punctuality, second for neatness, and third for discipline.

The assessment had started. In the first week, they kept adding sleeping pills to my milk. I used to drink it at night. I was late for all the classes. In the second week, they destroyed my project and in the third, they replaced my notes with teachers' funny drawings.

In the end, Mitalya won the award. When I got to know that I wasn't late to the classes by mistake, and they had planned to fail me in the assessment I had thought that I wanted revenge.

Four months later, I got employed at AVP Call Centre and when I knew they were also working there I had planned to take revenge. I even shifted to the nearest place to their homes, Deluxxe Apartments. I kept a strict eye on them and planned to steal the trophy, killing them wasn't a part of the plan. When I reached at Mitalya's house to steal the trophy, I saw her dead and even the trophy wasn't there. At some point I was happy that she was no more but still I wish I would have killed, not only her but the entire group- Amrita, Mitalya, Pragati and Natasha."

"What happened to you wasn't right but the stealing the trophy wasn't the right way either. Well, I think this was God's way to keep you away from doing something wrong," said Hina.

"Yes, and you should have informed the teachers back then, when you knew that Mitalya won by cheating" stated Dev.

"I couldn't, they would not have believed me if I did, I did not have any proof," she mourned.

"Even if you would have stolen the trophy, what use it would be to you? Mitalya had already won it at college," said Lakshman.

"And there were many other legal ways to get your trophy back, I am glad that your plan of stealing the trophy didn't work" stated Priya.

"Look, now I have told you. Take me to the hospital, otherwise, I'll die" she sobbed and ran towards the door.

Priya caught her and compelled her to sit again.

"That was just a trick to extract the confession," said Hina.

"That means you lied to me" she fumed.

"Yes, but tell me how come we found Mahesh, Shyam, Akshay and Anupam's photos at your house?" asked Dev.

"And what about the empty bottle of arsenic that was found at your house?" continued Hina.

"Even that would be planned, go and ask Mahesh and Shyam about all this, I don't know," she answered.

"Yes, we will surely ask them" Hina clenched her fists.

"Can I leave now?" asked Akanksha.

"You will be under custody until we find the criminal," commanded Dev and he followed Hina who left in anger after getting to know that Mahesh and Shyam lied to them. Lakshman and Priya followed him.

CHAPTER FOURTEEN

Hina headed towards the prison furiously, she kicked open the door and got inside. Mahesh and Shyam who were sitting, stood up in fear when they heard the noise. Dev, Priya, and Lakshman rushed towards the prison and saw her inside.

"Her anger is on peak, go stop her" whispered Dev.

"N..no, Hina ma'am's anger is inflamed right now, I cannot put my life on risk" mumbled Lakshman.

"Yes…sir, he is right. You are the only one who can stop her. Please…" Priya requested Dev.

"I think she will handle them; she is an expert in extracting confessions. If something goes out of hand, then I will step inside" he said.

Meanwhile Hina held their wrists, pulled them, twisted their hands, and pinned them to wall.

"Aahh…" they winced in pain.

"Who gave you the contract to kill Mitalya and Pragati?" she demanded.

"Aaaa…Akanksha…." stammered Mahesh.

"Oh! Let us see today how much you can lie" she fumed, making her grip tighter and pushing them to wall even more.

"We…we are not ly…lying….," stuttered Shyam.

"Oh my," sighed Dev. "Just tell the truth and save your lives. It is that easy," he commanded.

Hina gave him a deadly look.

"Did I say something wrong?" he mumbled.

"No," she focused on Mahesh and Shyam, "I guess you also listened to what he said, it's that easy, just tell the truth"

"We have told you the truth already," they said in a breath.

"Oh really," Dev stepped inside.

Hina took out her gun and slid it from their forehead to face and then rested it above Mahesh's ear. They both were horrified after feeling the gun on their face and her grip was even tighter than before. They were pinned to wall with the gun on Mahesh's face.

"You have only ten seconds, either tell the truth or the bullet will travel through your brains. Mahesh, I will just shoot you. The gun is so close that the bullet will even travel through Shyam's brain," she fumed.

"One…two…," Dev started their time.

Mahesh and Shyam exchanged looks.

"Three...four...," continued Priya.

"Five…. six…," added Lakshman.

"Seven…. eight…., and it's just the end of your life in two more seconds" stated Hina about to press the trigger.

Mahesh and Shyam nodded and yelled, "Wait,"

Hina removed her finger from the trigger.

"We will tell the truth, please don't kill us," they requested.

"Are you sure?" Hina confirmed.

"Yes, yes absolutely" they answered.

Hina removed the gun from Mahesh's face and kept it back into her coat.

"Speak up who gave you the contract to kill Mitalya and Pragati?" demanded Hina.

They looked at Dev and he looked at her.

"What?" she asked Dev.

"Leave them, how will they speak" he answered.

"Oh Okay," she left them.

"Aaaahhh….," they winced.

Priya and Lakshman stepped inside, Hina saw them with a questioning look on her face.

"Why were you standing outside?" she asked.

They looked at Dev with a confusing face, asking him what to say. Dev changes the topic, "Leave that, you both tell the truth now" he stated.

"Yes, tell the truth," continued Hina.

"Someone from AVP Call Centre forced us to take the name of Akanksha in case you arrest us," said Shyam.

"And you agreed," stated Lakshman.

"Well, who is that someone?" questioned Priya.

"We had to agree, there was no other option. A lady from AVP Call Centre blackmailed us that she will kill our families if we don't do what she asks us to," answered Mahesh.

"So, are you the one who put the keyring under Mitalya's bed and kept an empty bottle of arsenic and photos of you both including Anupam and Akshaya at Akanksha's house?" asked Dev.

"Yes, that lady asked us to do so. So that every proof is against Akanksha," responded Shyam.

"Who is that lady?" questioned Hina.

"We don't know," replied Mahesh.

"Have you seen her?" interrogated Priya.

"Yes," answered Shyam.

"Okay, then help us in getting her sketch ready," ordered Priya. They called the sketch artist and Mahesh and Shyam were asked to describe her appearance.

They got back in the bureau and decided to leave Akanksha as Mahesh and Shyam had accepted that all the evidence against her were planned. They move towards Akanksha.

"You can leave now," said Hina.

"Really!" she exclaimed.

"Yes, you are proved innocent. Every evidence was planned," stated Dev,

"But who's the real criminal?" she asked.

"That's our work, we only know that there is a lady from AVP Call Centre" replied Dev.

"Yes. Do something better with your life instead of holding grudges and taking revenges" said Hina.

"Okay," stated Akanksha and she left.

CHAPTER FIFTEEN

The next day

"Priya, do we have the sketch ready?" asked Hina.

"Yes ma'am" she handed the sketch to Hina.

"Oh! So, we found our criminal" she said looking at the sketch.

"Yes, let's arrest her then" stated Dev taking a glimpse at the sketch.

They drove to AVP Call Centre and stepped inside.

"Did you arrest the criminal?" asked Swati.

"No, we just found her and here we are to arrest her," answered Dev.

"'HER', that means the criminal is a girl?" she asked.

"Exactly," replied Hina.

"Lakshman, close the doors. So that no one is able to step outside" ordered Priya.

"Sure," he agreed and closed the doors.

"But who is the criminal?" asked Swati.

"Wait, have some patience" answered Dev.

Suddenly the lights went off, it was all dark everyone started panicking.

"Don't panic," stated Hina. "The lights will be back in a minute, and we will also find our criminal," she continued.

The spotlight was on a girl, Priya held her arm and made her stand in front of Hina. The lights were back. Everyone was looking at the girl.

"What? Why am I here? I am not the criminal" said the girl in one go.

"Oh really! I guess then your spirit gave the contract to Mahesh and Shyam for killing Mitalya and Pragati, and Anupam and Akshay to put Aconite leaves in Natasha's bouquet and Arsenic in Amrita's water. The list isn't short, you also blackmailed Mahesh and Shyam that you will harm their families if they didn't listen to you. You are the one who tried to trap Akanksha in all this fuss," fumed Hina.

The girl tried to run but Hina caught her by collar.

"No girl. There's no chance to escape now," she said, turning and handcuffing her.

When she turned her Swati saw her face and she was disappointed.

"Zoya! I never thought you would kill our employees and do such a sin. You are fired," she thundered.

"But ma'am—"

"Shut up!" she shouted.

"Now would you please tell the truth, or—" said Hina.

"Yes, I am telling the truth." She sobbed as she understood what Hina meant.

They bought a chair and compelled her to sit.

"What made you hire four different people to kill Amrita, Natasha, Pragati and Mitalya? Why did you drag Akanksha in all this?" demanded Dev.

"Once, in a presentation I got bitterly scolded by Swati ma'am because of these four girls, which ruined my image. Turned out that they made changes in my presentation in order to let me down. Pragati always wanted to be the manager and take my place. She always thought that I did not deserve to be the manager. When I found out that all of them were involved in this bluff, I decided to take revenge and planned to hire four different people for murdering them," narrated Zoya.

"And what about Akanksha? Why did you drag her in the fuss you created?" asked Hina.

"I overheard her when she was talking to someone on the phone about how Mitalya won the trophy at college by cheating and Pragati, Amrita and Natasha helped her. She also stated that she was going to steal the trophy from Mitalya's home at night. So, I asked Mahesh and Shyam to steal that trophy and drop a keyring with the letter 'A' under Mitalya's bed. The empty arsenic bottle which you found from Akanksha's house was kept by Mahesh as per my instructions. I blackmailed them that I will harm their families if they didn't listen to me and take Akanksha's name in case they get arrested. So, that you can easily believe that Akanksha is the culprit, and I would be safe once the case was closed" she continued.

"Wow! What a plan! This would be successful if Mahesh and Shyam would not tell us the truth...," said Dev.

"But oops! Your plan failed," said Hina. "You took the wrong decision in anger. Your ego brought you to the noose," she fumed.

"Do you consider yourself as a hero after murdering four people and trying to trap the innocent? This is not an act of bravery!" thundered Dev.

"Do you have the trophy which Mahesh and Shyam stole from Mitalya's house?" questioned Lakshman.

"Yes," she said looking down on the floor guiltily.

"Lakshman, the trophy should be in the bureau in an hour" ordered Priya.

"Okay ma'am," he followed.

"Shame on you!" shouted Swati.

"Four murders, blackmailing Mahesh and Shyam, and for trapping an innocent. You will be hanged to death!" stated Hina.

Crime Unit arrested Zoya and put her behind the bars, till they got the orders from the High court that she will be hanged to death. The trophy was handed to Mitalya's parents. Akanksha did not indulge in any wrong activity after this case.

CASE CLOSED

*****

PRANJAL VERMA

Pranjal is a 13-year-old young writer. She discovered her love for writing in Covid-19 lockdown, this is her first book. She also writes poetry and short stories. She is enthusiastic about art and also has an art page on Instagram @artist_pranjal. Being an avid reader, she is a huge fan of crime fiction and thrillers.

INKFEATHERS PUBLISHING

India's Most Author Friendly Publishing House

Stay updated about the latest books, anthologies, events, exclusive offers, contests, product giveaways and other things that we do to support authors.

f Inkfeathers Publishing

⊙ @InkfeathersPublishing

🐦 @_Inkfeathers

in @Inkfeathes

🌐 Inkfeathers.com

We'd love to connect with you!